BLIND JUSTICE

III

A Beacom of Hope

Dr. Maxwell Shimba

Printed by Shimba Publishing LLC
Printed in the United States of America

First Printing Edition, 2024

TABLE OF CONTENTS

PREFACE

In the quest for justice, the line between right and wrong often becomes blurred, and the path to truth is seldom straightforward. "Blind Justice III: The Dawn of a New Era" is the third volume in a series that delves into the complexities of morality, integrity, and the relentless pursuit of what is right. This book continues the journey of Detective Alex Turner and lawyer Sarah Miller as they navigate the treacherous waters of corruption and deceit, striving to uphold justice in a world where it is often compromised.

The first volume introduced readers to the challenges faced by Alex and Sarah as they confronted a web of deceit and corruption that threatened to engulf their community. The second volume deepened their struggle, illustrating the heavy burden that comes with the pursuit of justice and the personal sacrifices that it demands. In this third installment, we see our protagonists at the brink of transformation, having faced down formidable adversaries and emerged with a renewed commitment to their mission.

"Blind Justice III: The Dawn of a New Era" explores the aftermath of their hard-fought battles and the new challenges that arise as they continue their quest. This volume is not just a continuation of their story, but a testament to the enduring spirit of those who fight for justice. It delves into the personal growth of Alex and Sarah, the evolution of their ideals, and the impact they have on the community they serve.

Throughout this series, the theme of justice as a multifaceted and ever-evolving concept is prevalent. Justice is not merely about the letter of the law, but about the spirit in which it is enforced. It is about standing up for the marginalized, giving voice to the voiceless, and challenging the status quo. Alex and Sarah's journey is a reflection of these ideals, showcasing their resilience in the face of adversity and their unwavering belief in the power of truth.

This volume also introduces new characters and unforeseen challenges, expanding the narrative to include diverse perspectives and highlighting the interconnectedness of society. It is a reminder that justice is not the responsibility of a few, but a collective effort that requires the participation and vigilance of all.

As you embark on this journey with Alex and Sarah, you will be drawn into a world where the stakes are high and the outcomes are uncertain. You will witness their struggles, their triumphs, and the lessons they learn along the way. "Blind Justice III: The Dawn of a New Era" is a story of hope, resilience, and the unyielding pursuit of justice, a beacon for all who believe in the possibility of a better, more just world.

We invite you to join Alex and Sarah as they continue their fight, knowing that their story is a reflection of the broader human experience—a testament to the enduring power of justice and the belief that, despite the obstacles, the truth will always prevail.

— Dr. Maxwell Shimba

DR. MAXWELL SHIMBA

CHAPTER 01

THE SILENT WITNESS

The city of Centerton, with its gleaming skyscrapers and bustling streets, had always been a place of contrasts. Beneath the surface of its vibrant exterior lay a complex web of secrets, corruption, and untold stories. Detective Alex Turner and lawyer Sarah Miller had faced many challenges in their pursuit of justice, but nothing could have prepared them for the case that now lay before them.

It began on a cold, gray morning when Alex received a call from his old friend, Officer Jim Rodriguez. Jim's voice, usually calm and measured, was tinged with urgency and unease.

"Alex, we need you at the old warehouse on the east side. We've got a witness, but... there's a complication."

Alex arrived at the scene to find a group of officers standing around a young woman, her eyes wide with fear. She was clutching a small notebook to her chest, her hands trembling. Jim approached Alex, his expression grim.

"Her name is Emily Harper. She witnessed something, something big. But she's mute. She can't speak, and she's clearly traumatized."

Sarah joined them shortly after, her keen eyes assessing the situation. "Let's get her somewhere safe," she suggested, her voice soothing. "We need to understand what she's seen."

Emily was taken to a secure location, where Alex and Sarah began the delicate process of unraveling her story. Communication was a challenge, but Sarah's empathy and patience made a significant difference. Using a combination of written notes, drawings, and gestures, Emily began to share the fragments of the nightmarish event she had witnessed.

Piece by piece, Alex and Sarah assembled the puzzle. Emily had been at the warehouse the night before, working late as a janitor when she stumbled upon a clandestine meeting between several high-profile figures in the city. Through her drawings, she revealed faces that Alex and Sarah recognized: politicians, business tycoons, and even a few law enforcement officers. They were engaged in a heated discussion, exchanging envelopes and making sinister plans.

The more Emily revealed the more Alex and Sarah realized the magnitude of what they were dealing with. This wasn't just a simple crime; it was a conspiracy that stretched far beyond what they could have imagined. The implications were staggering, threatening to unravel the very fabric of their community.

Their investigation led them into a labyrinth of deceit and corruption. Each step forward was met with resistance and danger. They encountered bribed officials, forged documents, and threats meant to deter them from pursuing the truth. But Alex and Sarah were relentless. They knew that Emily's life was at risk, and so was the integrity of their city.

As they delved deeper, they uncovered a sinister plot involving money laundering, illegal land deals, and a scheme to manipulate the upcoming city elections. The conspirators had woven a tight web of corruption, one that had ensnared many of the city's most influential figures.

One evening, as Alex pored over the evidence in his office, Sarah arrived with a new lead. "We have a name," she said, her voice determined. "Daniel Grant. He's the linchpin. If we can get to him, we can unravel this entire conspiracy."

Daniel Grant was a wealthy real estate developer with connections to some of the most powerful people in Centerton. He had managed to stay out of the spotlight, but Emily's testimony and the evidence they had gathered pointed directly to him as the mastermind behind the corruption.

With this new lead, Alex and Sarah devised a plan to bring Daniel Grant to justice. They knew it wouldn't be easy. He had resources and influence far beyond what they could muster, but they also had the truth on their side—and the unwavering determination to see justice served.

As they prepared for the final showdown, Emily's courage became their guiding light. Her willingness to come forward, despite her fear and inability to speak, inspired them to push forward, no matter the cost.

The pursuit of truth took on a new urgency as Alex and Sarah raced against time. The web of deceit they had uncovered was vast, but they were determined to dismantle it, thread by thread. The silent witness, Emily Harper, had given them the key to a case that would change Centerton forever.

As they moved forward, they knew that the journey would be fraught with challenges. But they also knew that justice, once set in motion, could not be silenced. And with Emily's story as their beacon, they were prepared to face whatever came next, united in their unwavering commitment to unveiling the truth and bringing the perpetrators to justice.

CHAPTER 02

THE WIGHT OF TRUTH

The weight of the truth bore down heavily on Detective Alex Turner and lawyer Sarah Miller as they delved deeper into the case. Each new piece of evidence they uncovered painted an increasingly grim picture of Centerton—a city rife with corruption and injustice, where the powerful preyed on the weak with impunity.

Alex sat in his office, staring at a wall covered in photographs, maps, and notes. Strings connected the pieces of evidence, forming a complex web that mirrored the one they were trying to untangle. He rubbed his temples, feeling the burden of the knowledge they had acquired. The corruption they were uncovering wasn't just a series of isolated incidents; it was a systemic rot that had infected every level of the city's governance.

Sarah walked in, holding a stack of files. "I just finished going through Emily's notebook again," she said, placing the files on Alex's desk. "There are more names, more connections. It's worse than we thought."

Alex looked up, his eyes heavy with the gravity of their situation. "Every time we think we've reached the bottom, it goes deeper," he said. "This isn't just about a few bad actors. It's the whole system."

They reviewed the latest evidence together. The files contained financial records, emails, and secret contracts that revealed a staggering level of corruption. Politicians were being bribed, city officials were turning a blind eye, and businesses were exploiting the system for their own gain. The powerful elite of Centerton were intertwined in a web of deceit, each protecting the other while the common citizens suffered.

One name kept resurfacing in their investigation: Daniel Grant. He was the nexus of this corruption, the linchpin holding the entire scheme together. But bringing him down would not be easy. He was protected by layers of loyal subordinates, many of whom were willing to do anything to keep their secrets hidden.

Sarah sighed, leaning back in her chair. "The more we uncover, the more I realize how much damage they've done. Lives ruined, opportunities stolen... it's heartbreaking."

Alex nodded. "And it's not just about catching the bad guys. It's about restoring faith in the system. People need to believe that justice can prevail."

As they continued their investigation, they began to see the human cost of the corruption. They met with victims—families who had lost their homes to fraudulent real estate schemes, small business owners pushed out by unfair regulations, and honest city workers who had been fired for refusing to participate in illegal activities. Each story added to the weight they carried, reinforcing their determination to see this case through to the end.

One evening, Alex and Sarah visited a neighborhood that had been particularly hard hit by Grant's schemes. They walked through streets lined with boarded-up houses and abandoned businesses. The community had been vibrant once, but now it was a ghost town, its residents displaced and its spirit broken.

They met Maria Hernandez, a former teacher who had become a community organizer after losing her home to a predatory lending scheme. Maria's eyes were filled with anger and sadness as she recounted her story. "They took everything from us," she said. "Our homes, our livelihoods, our sense of security. And they did it because they knew they could get away with it."

Sarah took Maria's hand. "We're going to make sure they don't get away with it any longer. We're going to bring them to justice."

Maria nodded, tears in her eyes. "Thank you. We need people like you to fight for us."

As they left the neighborhood, Alex and Sarah felt the weight of their mission more acutely than ever. The pursuit of justice was no longer just a professional duty; it had become a moral imperative. They were fighting for the soul of their city, for the countless innocent people who had been trampled by the powerful and corrupt.

In the days that followed, they worked tirelessly, pushing themselves to their limits. Every new piece of evidence, every new connection, brought them closer to their goal but also deepened the sense of responsibility they felt. They knew that exposing the truth would have far-reaching consequences, and they were prepared to face whatever challenges lay ahead.

As they moved forward, Alex and Sarah found strength in their partnership and in the support of those who believed in their mission. The weight of truth was heavy, but it was also a powerful motivator, driving them to confront the harsh realities of their world and to shape a future where justice could prevail.

In the heart of Centerton, where shadows of corruption loomed large, Detective Alex Turner and lawyer Sarah Miller stood resolute. Their pursuit of justice was no longer just about solving a case—it was about reclaiming their city from those who had sought to corrupt it. And as long as they had breath in their bodies, they would continue to fight, knowing that the weight of truth, though heavy, was a burden worth bearing.

CHAPTER 03

SHADOWS OF THE DOUBT

The relentless pursuit of justice had taken its toll on Detective Alex Turner and lawyer Sarah Miller. The weight of the truths they had uncovered pressed down on them, and the complexity of the case at hand seemed insurmountable. As they navigated the labyrinth of corruption and deceit, doubt began to creep into their minds.

It started subtly at first, a whisper of uncertainty that echoed in the quiet moments when Alex sat alone in his office, staring at the evidence board. He found himself questioning his own beliefs and assumptions. Was their fight really making a difference? Could they ever hope to dismantle the deeply entrenched systems of power and corruption?

Sarah felt it too. During the long nights of poring over documents and re-interviewing witnesses, she found herself wondering if they were truly making progress or if they were merely chasing shadows. The moral clarity that had once driven her seemed to blur as the lines between right and wrong grew increasingly convoluted.

One evening, after a particularly grueling day, Alex and Sarah met at their usual spot—a small, dimly lit café that had become their refuge. They sat in silence for a while, nursing their coffees, each lost in their own thoughts.

"Do you ever wonder if we're doing the right thing?" Alex finally asked, breaking the silence. His voice was weary, laden with the weight of their shared burden.

Sarah looked at him, her eyes reflecting the same doubts. "All the time," she admitted. "Sometimes I feel like we're just scratching the surface, and for every victory we achieve, there are a dozen more battles waiting for us. It feels endless."

Alex nodded, staring into his cup. "We've uncovered so much, but it still feels like we're not making a dent. The corruption runs so deep. Sometimes I wonder if it's worth the cost—our time, our energy, our peace of mind."

They both knew the toll their work had taken on their personal lives. Alex's relationship with his father remained strained, and Sarah struggled to balance her responsibilities as a mother with the demands of the case. The pursuit of justice had come with sacrifices, and the cost was becoming increasingly clear.

"But we can't give up," Sarah said, her voice firmer now. "We owe it to people like Emily and Maria. We've seen the damage that's been done, and we have a responsibility to try and fix it. Even if it's just a small part."

Alex sighed. "You're right. But it's hard not to feel overwhelmed. Every step forward feels like we're dragging a mountain behind us."

Sarah reached across the table and placed her hand on Alex's. "I know. But remember why we started this. We're not just fighting for justice in the abstract. We're fighting for real people, for their lives and their futures. And every bit of progress we make, no matter how small, is a victory for them."

As they sat there, they began to confront their doubts head-on. They realized that the pursuit of truth was not just about exposing corruption or bringing perpetrators to justice.

It was also a journey of self-discovery, one that required them to confront their own biases and preconceptions.

They had to acknowledge that their fight was not going to be easy or straightforward. The road ahead was fraught with challenges, and there would be times when they would feel like giving up. But they also knew that the pursuit of justice was a noble endeavor, one that demanded perseverance and resilience.

In the days that followed, Alex and Sarah recommitted themselves to their mission. They approached their work with renewed determination, drawing strength from each other and from the people they were fighting for. They understood that doubt was a natural part of the journey, but it was not an insurmountable obstacle.

They began to see their doubts not as weaknesses, but as opportunities for growth. By questioning their beliefs and assumptions, they were able to refine their approach and deepen their understanding of the complexities they were facing. The pursuit of truth required them to be adaptable, to learn from their experiences, and to remain steadfast in their commitment to justice.

In the heart of Centerton, where shadows of doubt loomed large, Detective Alex Turner and lawyer Sarah Miller stood united. Their journey was far from over, but they were ready to face whatever challenges lay ahead. They knew that the pursuit of truth was a path of self-discovery, one that required them to confront their own fears and uncertainties. And as long as they continued to fight for what was right, they would find the strength to overcome any obstacle.

The shadows of doubt had tested them, but they had emerged stronger, more resolute, and more determined than ever to see justice prevail.

CHAPTER 04

THE BURDEN OF PROOF

The day of the trial was fast approaching, and the burden of proof weighed heavily on Detective Alex Turner and lawyer Sarah Miller. They had spent countless hours gathering evidence, interviewing witnesses, and piecing together the intricate web of corruption that had ensnared Centerton. Now, they stood on the precipice of presenting their case, knowing that the evidence they had uncovered was both damning and precarious.

In the days leading up to the trial, Alex and Sarah worked tirelessly to prepare their arguments and ensure that their evidence was irrefutable. They knew they would face fierce opposition from powerful adversaries determined to protect their interests. The courtroom would become a battleground where the truth had to be fought for with every ounce of their strength and determination.

The morning of the trial dawned clear and cold. Alex arrived at the courthouse early, his mind racing with thoughts of the upcoming battle. He knew that their case hinged on the credibility of their evidence and the testimony of key witnesses like Emily Harper and Maria Hernandez. The stakes were higher than ever, and failure was not an option.

Sarah joined him shortly after, carrying a stack of files and a determined look in her eyes. "Are you ready for this?" she asked, her voice steady despite the tension that hung in the air.

"As ready as I'll ever be," Alex replied, taking a deep breath. "Let's do this."

The courtroom buzzed with anticipation as they entered. Journalists, spectators, and members of the community filled the seats, eager to witness the unfolding drama. The defense team, representing the powerful figures they sought to bring to justice, was already seated, exuding an air of confidence and superiority.

As the trial began, Sarah took the lead, presenting the opening statements with eloquence and precision. She laid out the case, detailing the corruption, bribery, and illegal activities that had plagued Centerton. She emphasized the human cost of these actions, highlighting the stories of victims like Emily and Maria.

The defense attorney, a slick and seasoned litigator named Robert Blake, countered with equal fervor. He sought to discredit the witnesses and cast doubt on the integrity of the evidence. His strategy was clear: sow seeds of uncertainty and protect his clients at all costs.

The burden of proof was a heavy mantle, and Sarah felt its weight with every word she spoke. She called Emily Harper to the stand, her heart pounding as the young woman took her place. Emily, though mute, had prepared a written testimony and would communicate through a sign language interpreter.

As Emily recounted the night she had witnessed the clandestine meeting, the courtroom fell silent. Her testimony was compelling, painting a vivid picture of the corruption she had stumbled upon. Sarah presented corroborating evidence—financial records, emails, and photographs—that linked the defendants to the crimes.

Robert Blake attacked her credibility, suggesting that Emily's trauma had clouded her memory and that her testimony was unreliable. He questioned the validity of the evidence, insinuating that it had been manipulated.

Sarah remained composed, countering each of Blake's arguments with facts and logic. She knew that the burden of proof lay on their shoulders, and she was determined to bear it with unwavering resolve.

Next, Maria Hernandez took the stand. Her testimony was equally powerful, detailing the impact of the corruption on her community. She spoke of the predatory lending schemes, the loss of homes, and the devastation wrought by the greed of the powerful.

Blake attempted to discredit Maria as well, but her strength and conviction shone through. Sarah supported her testimony with additional evidence, building a compelling case that left little room for doubt.

As the trial progressed, Alex and Sarah faced one challenge after another. The defense called witnesses to refute their claims, presenting alternative explanations and casting aspersions on their motives. It was a relentless battle, with each side fighting tooth and nail for the truth.

In the moments of doubt and uncertainty, Alex and Sarah drew strength from their unwavering belief in their mission. They knew that the pursuit of justice was never easy and that the burden of proof was a heavy but necessary weight. They remained steadfast, their resolve unshaken by the opposition's tactics.

The climax of the trial came when Sarah delivered her closing arguments. She spoke from the heart, her words a passionate plea for justice. She reminded the jury of the evidence they had seen, the testimonies they had heard, and the undeniable truth that lay at the core of their case.

"Justice is not just about the law," she said, her voice resonating through the courtroom. "It's about doing what is right, standing up for those who cannot stand up for themselves, and ensuring that the powerful are held accountable for their actions. The burden of proof may be heavy, but the truth is clear. These defendants have committed grave injustices, and it is your duty to hold them accountable."

As the jury deliberated, Alex and Sarah waited with bated breath. The weight of their efforts, their sacrifices, and their unwavering commitment to justice hung in the balance.

When the verdict was finally delivered, it was a resounding affirmation of their work. The defendants were found guilty on multiple counts, and the courtroom erupted in a mixture of relief and triumph. Justice had prevailed, and the burden of proof had been borne with integrity and courage.

As Alex and Sarah left the courthouse, they felt a profound sense of accomplishment. The battle had been hard-fought, but the truth had won out. They knew that the fight for justice was far from over, but this victory was a testament to their resilience and determination.

In the heart of Centerton, where corruption had once thrived, a new chapter was being written—one where justice, though hard-won, was a beacon of hope and a testament to the power of truth. And as long as there were those who sought to undermine it, Alex and Sarah would be there, ready to bear the burden of proof and fight for what was right.

CHAPTER 05

ECHOES OF JUSTICE

The air in the courtroom was thick with anticipation as the trial reached its climax. The final days had been grueling, filled with intense cross-examinations, compelling testimonies, and a parade of evidence that painted a stark picture of corruption and betrayal. Detective Alex Turner and lawyer Sarah Miller stood at the epicenter of this storm, their belief in the power of truth driving them forward.

Alex and Sarah had spent countless hours preparing for this moment. They knew that the outcome of the trial would have far-reaching implications, not just for the defendants but for the entire community of Centerton. The pursuit of justice, once a deeply personal mission, had become a fight for the soul of the city.

The courtroom was packed, every seat taken by spectators, journalists, and members of the community who had come to witness the culmination of this landmark case. The air was charged with a mix of hope and apprehension, as people waited to see if justice would prevail.

Sarah took a deep breath as she prepared to deliver her closing arguments. She looked over at Alex, who gave her a reassuring nod. They had come so far, and now it was time to bring it all home.

"Your Honor, ladies and gentlemen of the jury," Sarah began, her voice steady and clear, "we have presented a case that lays bare the corruption and greed that have plagued our city. We have shown you evidence of bribery, fraud, and betrayal. But more importantly, we have shown you the human cost of these crimes. Lives have been ruined, families have been torn apart, and the very fabric of our community has been threatened."

She paused, letting her words sink in. The jury members were listening intently, their expressions serious and contemplative.

"The defendants in this case have wielded their power and influence to serve their own interests at the expense of others. They have preyed on the vulnerable, manipulated the system, and attempted to silence those who dared to stand against them. But today, we have the opportunity to say 'enough.' We have the chance to hold them accountable and to send a message that justice is not for sale."

Sarah's voice grew stronger, her passion evident in every word. "The pursuit of justice is not just about punishment; it is about restoring faith in our institutions and ensuring that no one is above the law. It is about giving a voice to the voiceless and standing up for those who cannot stand up for themselves."

She turned to the jury, her gaze unwavering. "We ask you to look at the evidence, to listen to the testimonies, and to consider the impact of your decision. The echoes of justice will reverberate far beyond this courtroom. They will be heard in the streets of Centerton, in the homes of its residents, and in the hearts of those who believe in the power of truth."

As Sarah concluded her argument, she felt a sense of calm wash over her. She had done everything she could to present their case, and now it was in the hands of the jury.

The defense attorney, Robert Blake, delivered his closing arguments with equal fervor, attempting to cast doubt on the evidence and paint the defendants as victims of a witch hunt. But Sarah could see that the jury was not swayed. They had seen the truth, and no amount of rhetoric could change that.

The judge gave the jury their instructions and sent them to deliberate. The tension in the courtroom was palpable as everyone waited for the verdict. Hours passed, each minute stretching into an eternity.

Finally, the jury returned. The foreperson stood, holding the piece of paper that would determine the fate of the defendants. The room fell silent as the judge asked for the verdict.

"On the count of conspiracy to commit fraud, we find the defendants guilty."

"On the count of bribery, we find the defendants guilty."

"On the count of corruption, we find the defendants guilty."

The echoes of justice reverberated through the courtroom as the verdict was read. There was a collective sigh of relief, followed by a ripple of applause and cheers from the spectators. The defendants sat in stunned silence, their expressions a mix of shock and resignation.

Alex and Sarah exchanged a look of triumph. They had done it. They had brought justice to Centerton and sent a powerful message that corruption and greed would not be tolerated.

As they left the courthouse, they were met with a wave of gratitude from the community. People thanked them, shook their hands, and expressed their relief that justice had been served. The fight for the soul of Centerton had been hard-fought, but it had been worth it.

In the days that followed, Alex and Sarah reflected on the journey they had taken. The pursuit of justice had tested them in ways they could never have imagined, but it had also strengthened their resolve and deepened their commitment to their cause.

The echoes of justice continued to reverberate through Centerton, inspiring others to stand up against corruption and fight for what was right. Alex and Sarah knew that their work was far from over, but they were ready to face whatever challenges lay ahead.

As they walked through the city they had fought so hard to protect, they felt a renewed sense of hope and determination. The pursuit of justice was a never-ending journey, but it was one they were willing to take, knowing that the power of truth would always prevail.

The fight for the soul of Centerton had been won, but the echoes of justice would continue to resonate, guiding them forward and inspiring others to join their cause.

CHAPTER 06

THE VERDICT

The courtroom buzzed with a tense anticipation that hung heavy in the air. The jury had been deliberating for hours, and every minute that ticked by felt like an eternity for Detective Alex Turner and lawyer Sarah Miller. They sat in silence, their thoughts racing, each absorbed in their own reflections on the journey that had brought them to this pivotal moment.

Alex glanced around the room, taking in the faces of the spectators who had followed the trial with rapt attention. There were journalists, community members, and even some of the victims of the corruption they had fought so hard to expose. Each face was a reminder of why they had embarked on this arduous pursuit of justice.

Sarah sat beside him, her hands folded in her lap, her gaze steady. She had been a beacon of strength and determination throughout the trial, and now, as they awaited the verdict, she felt a deep sense of calm. They had done everything they could, presented their case with integrity and passion, and now it was out of their hands.

"Remember why we started this," Sarah said quietly, breaking the silence. "No matter what happens, we've made a difference. We've given a voice to those who were silenced."

Alex nodded, his thoughts drifting back to the beginning of their journey. It had started with a simple investigation, a spark of suspicion that had led them down a path filled with danger and deceit. They had faced countless obstacles, from powerful adversaries to their own doubts, but they had persevered.

They thought of Emily Harper, the mute witness whose courage had been the catalyst for their investigation. Her silent testimony had spoken volumes, revealing the corruption that had festered beneath the surface of Centerton. They thought of Maria Hernandez, whose community had been devastated by the greed and betrayal of those in power. Their stories had fueled Alex and Sarah's determination, reminding them of the human cost of corruption and the importance of their fight for justice.

As they waited, Alex and Sarah reflected on the countless hours they had spent gathering evidence, interviewing witnesses, and preparing their case. They had uncovered a web of deceit that reached into the highest echelons of power, and they had brought it to light with unwavering resolve. The pursuit of truth had tested them in ways they could never have imagined, but it had also strengthened their bond and deepened their commitment to their cause.

Finally, the jury reentered the courtroom. The room fell silent as the judge called for order. The foreperson stood, holding the piece of paper that would determine the fate of the defendants. Alex and Sarah held their breath, their hearts pounding in their chests.

"Members of the jury, have you reached a verdict?" the judge asked.

"We have, Your Honor," the foreperson replied.

The foreperson began to read the verdict, each word resonating through the courtroom. "On the count of conspiracy to commit fraud, we find the defendants guilty. On the count of bribery, we find the defendants guilty. On the count of corruption, we find the defendants guilty."

A collective sigh of relief swept through the room, followed by a ripple of applause and cheers. The defendants sat in stunned silence, their expressions a mix of shock and resignation. Justice had been served.

Alex felt a wave of emotions wash over him—relief, triumph, and a deep sense of fulfillment. They had fought for the truth, and they had won. He glanced at Sarah, who met his gaze with a smile that spoke volumes. They had done it together, and the victory was all the sweeter for it.

As the courtroom emptied, Alex and Sarah remained seated, soaking in the moment. They knew that this was just one battle in a larger war against corruption, but it was a significant victory. They had proven that justice could prevail, even in the face of powerful adversaries and seemingly insurmountable odds.

"We did it," Alex said, his voice filled with quiet pride.

Sarah nodded. "Yes, we did. But our work isn't over. There are still so many who need our help, so many injustices that need to be addressed."

Alex agreed. "The fight for justice is a never-ending journey. But today, we've taken a big step forward."

As they left the courthouse, they were met with a wave of gratitude from the community. People thanked them, shook their hands, and expressed their relief that justice had been served. The fight for the soul of Centerton had been hard-fought, but it had been worth it.

In the days that followed, Alex and Sarah reflected on the journey that had brought them to this moment. The pursuit of truth had been long and arduous, filled with challenges and setbacks, but they had persevered. They knew that the fight for justice would continue, and they were ready to face whatever challenges lay ahead.

The verdict had reaffirmed their faith in the justice system and in their own ability to make a difference. They had proven that, with determination and integrity, it was possible to bring the powerful to account and restore faith in the institutions meant to protect and serve the people.

As they walked through the city they had fought so hard to protect, they felt a renewed sense of hope and determination. The pursuit of justice was a never-ending journey, but it was one they were willing to take, knowing that the power of truth would always prevail.

The fight for the soul of Centerton had been won, but the echoes of justice would continue to resonate, guiding them forward and inspiring others to join their cause.

CHAPTER 07

THE AFTERMATH

The courtroom was silent as the jury delivered their verdict. The defendants, who had once stood as titans of Centerton's elite, were now exonerated of the charges against them. Alex Turner and Sarah Miller sat in stunned disbelief, their minds reeling from the unexpected outcome.

"On the count of conspiracy to commit fraud, we find the defendants not guilty. On the count of bribery, we find the defendants not guilty. On the count of corruption, we find the defendants not guilty."

The words echoed in their ears, a stark contrast to the overwhelming evidence they had presented. How could this have happened? They had been so sure, so confident in their case. Now, they were left to grapple with the harsh reality of their defeat.

As the courtroom emptied, Alex and Sarah remained seated, trying to process the implications of the verdict. The defense team was already celebrating, shaking hands and exchanging triumphant smiles. For Alex and Sarah, the weight of their loss was palpable.

Sarah broke the silence first, her voice barely above a whisper. "How did this happen? We had everything—the evidence, the testimonies. It was all there."

Alex shook his head, his expression grim. "I don't know. Maybe the jury was influenced, maybe they were intimidated. Whatever the reason, it doesn't change the fact that we lost."

They left the courthouse in a daze, the cold air outside doing little to clear their minds. The community members who had supported them, who had hoped for justice, now looked at them with a mixture of disappointment and sympathy. It was a bitter pill to swallow.

In the days that followed, Alex and Sarah struggled to come to terms with their defeat. They had poured their hearts and souls into the case, believing that they could make a difference. Now, it felt like all their efforts had been for nothing.

Alex spent long hours in his office, going over the evidence again and again, searching for any missed detail that could explain the verdict. Sarah, meanwhile, found solace in her family, but the weight of their failure hung heavy on her shoulders.

One evening, as they sat together in the small café that had become their refuge, Sarah spoke up. "We can't let this defeat define us. We knew going into this that it wouldn't be easy. Justice isn't always about winning in the courtroom."

Alex looked at her, his eyes tired but resolute. "You're right. It's about standing up for what's right, no matter the cost. We may have lost this battle, but the war isn't over."

Sarah nodded. "We have to keep fighting. For Emily, for Maria, for everyone who has suffered because of these corrupt individuals. Our work isn't done."

Their conversation was a turning point. They realized that the pursuit of justice was not just about securing convictions—it was about shining a light on corruption, giving a voice to the voiceless, and standing up for what was right, even in the face of defeat.

Determined to move forward, Alex and Sarah redoubled their efforts. They reached out to their allies in the community, sharing their findings and encouraging others to join the fight against corruption. They held meetings, organized rallies, and worked to raise awareness about the issues that had plagued Centerton for so long.

Slowly but surely, they began to see the impact of their efforts. More people came forward with stories of corruption and injustice, emboldened by Alex and Sarah's courage. The media picked up on their work, shining a spotlight on the issues they had uncovered and holding those in power accountable.

Despite the verdict, they found strength in the support of their community. They realized that justice was not a destination but a journey—one that required perseverance, resilience, and an unwavering commitment to the truth.

In time, they saw changes. Some of the individuals they had exposed faced investigations and repercussions, and the pressure on the city's leaders to address corruption grew. It was a slow process, but it was progress nonetheless.

Alex and Sarah understood that their fight for justice would never truly end. There would always be new challenges, new battles to fight. But they were ready to face them, knowing that their work made a difference, even if it wasn't always reflected in the courtroom.

As they continued their journey, they carried with them the lessons they had learned. The pursuit of justice was not just about winning cases—it was about standing up for what was right, no matter the cost. And as long as they remained committed to that principle, they knew they would never truly be defeated.

The aftermath of the trial had left them reeling, but it had also made them stronger. They had faced their doubts and fears, and come out the other side with a renewed sense of purpose. The fight for justice was far from over, and Alex Turner and Sarah Miller were more determined than ever to see it through.

CHAPTER 08

NEW BEGINNINGS

The echoes of their recent defeat still lingered in the back of their minds, but Detective Alex Turner and lawyer Sarah Miller knew they couldn't afford to dwell on the past. The fight for justice in Centerton was far from over, and they were more determined than ever to make a difference. The verdict may not have been what they had hoped for, but it had only strengthened their resolve.

With the support of their community and each other, Alex and Sarah decided it was time to embark on a new chapter in their lives—one that would be defined by perseverance, resilience, and an unwavering commitment to the truth.

On a crisp morning, Alex and Sarah sat together in their small, familiar café, discussing their plans. The warm sunlight streamed through the windows, casting a hopeful glow over their faces.

"We can't let this setback define us," Sarah said, her eyes filled with determination. "We have to keep moving forward, keep fighting for what's right. The people of Centerton need us."

Alex nodded, taking a sip of his coffee. "Agreed. We need to regroup, re-strategize, and find new ways to tackle the corruption and injustice in our city. This isn't the end—it's just the beginning of a new chapter."

They decided to expand their efforts beyond the courtroom. They would work to build a coalition of like-minded individuals and organizations dedicated to fighting corruption and advocating for justice. It would be a grassroots movement, one that would empower the community and create lasting change.

Their first step was to reach out to their allies—journalists, activists, community leaders, and concerned citizens. They organized a meeting at the local community center, inviting everyone who had a stake in the fight against corruption.

On the evening of the meeting, the community center buzzed with activity. People from all walks of life filled the room, their faces reflecting a mix of hope and determination. Alex and Sarah stood at the front, ready to address the crowd.

"Thank you all for coming," Sarah began, her voice steady and confident. "We may have faced a setback in the courtroom, but our fight for justice is far from over. We are here to start something new, something powerful. Together, we can create a movement that will bring about real change in Centerton."

Alex stepped forward, his presence commanding attention. "We've seen the impact of corruption firsthand. We've seen how it destroys lives and undermines our community. But we also know that we have the power to fight back. This is our city, and it's up to us to protect it."

The room erupted in applause, and Alex and Sarah could see the fire of determination in the eyes of their audience. It was clear that they were not alone in their fight—there were many who shared their vision and were ready to stand alongside them.

Over the next few weeks, Alex and Sarah worked tirelessly to build their coalition. They organized rallies and workshops, educating the community about the signs of corruption and how to combat it. They created a network of whistleblowers and informants, providing them with the tools and support they needed to expose wrongdoing.

They also launched a public awareness campaign, using social media, local newspapers, and radio to spread their message. The response was overwhelming. People from all corners of Centerton came forward, sharing their stories and pledging their support.

As their movement gained momentum, Alex and Sarah began to see the impact of their efforts. Local officials and business leaders, once confident in their impunity, now faced increased scrutiny and accountability. Investigations were launched, and some of the corrupt practices they had uncovered were brought to light.

One afternoon, as Alex and Sarah reviewed their progress, they received a visit from Emily Harper. Her face was a mixture of gratitude and determination.

"I wanted to thank you," Emily signed through her interpreter. "Because of you, people are listening. People are fighting back. You gave me the courage to stand up, and now I see that I'm not alone."

Sarah smiled warmly. "Thank you, Emily. Your bravery has been an inspiration to all of us. This is just the beginning, and together, we will continue to make a difference."

As Emily left, Alex turned to Sarah. "We've come a long way, haven't we? There's still so much work to do, but I feel like we're finally making progress."

Sarah nodded. "Yes, we are. And it's because we're not just fighting for justice in the courtroom—we're fighting for it in our community, in our everyday lives. This is what true justice looks like."

Their journey was far from over, but Alex and Sarah were ready for whatever challenges lay ahead. They had faced setbacks and defeats, but they had also found new strength and determination. With the support of their community and their unwavering commitment to the truth, they knew they could create lasting change.

As they stood side by side, looking out over the city they had sworn to protect, they felt a renewed sense of purpose. The road ahead would be difficult, but they were ready to face it together.

In the heart of Centerton, a new beginning had taken root. The fight for justice was far from over, but Alex Turner and Sarah Miller were more determined than ever to see it through. Their journey had only just begun, and they were ready to make a difference—one step at a time.

CHAPTER 09

THE UNSEEN HAND

The momentum of their newfound movement gave Alex Turner and Sarah Miller a renewed sense of purpose. They had galvanized the community and begun to see the fruits of their labor. However, just as they were beginning to make significant strides, a new and insidious adversary emerged from the shadows, threatening to undermine their efforts.

This unseen hand operated with a level of sophistication and secrecy that Alex and Sarah had not encountered before. Subtle manipulations of events, mysterious setbacks, and inexplicable shifts in public opinion pointed to a hidden force working against them. It was clear that someone—or some group—was intent on preserving the status quo of corruption and power.

Their first indication of this new threat came in the form of a seemingly innocuous rumor that began circulating through the community. It suggested that Alex and Sarah's efforts were not genuinely aimed at justice but were instead a ploy for political power. The rumor spread quickly, sowing seeds of doubt and mistrust among their supporters.

One evening, as Alex and Sarah met to discuss their next steps, Sarah's phone buzzed with a notification. She frowned as she read the message. "Alex, take a look at this," she said, handing him her phone. It was an article from a local blog, accusing them of using their movement for personal gain.

Alex's brow furrowed as he read. "This is complete nonsense. We need to find out who's behind this."

Their investigation led them to a maze of anonymous sources and shadowy figures, all leading back to a single, elusive entity. This unseen hand seemed to be everywhere and nowhere, pulling strings and manipulating events with a deftness that made it difficult to trace.

As they dug deeper, they encountered obstacles at every turn. Their computers were hacked, key witnesses recanted their statements, and documents went missing. It was as if their every move was being watched and countered. The adversary they faced was highly skilled and had resources at their disposal that Alex and Sarah could scarcely imagine.

The turning point came when they received a tip from an unexpected source. Marcus Rodriguez, the reformed ex-convict who had become one of their most reliable allies, approached them with crucial information.

"I've been hearing things on the street," Marcus said, his expression serious. "There's someone new in town. Goes by the name 'The Broker.' No one knows who they really are, but they're the one orchestrating all of this."

"The Broker?" Sarah repeated. "What do we know about them?"

"Not much," Marcus admitted. "They're like a ghost. But they have connections everywhere—in business, politics, even law enforcement. They're playing a long game, and we're the pawns."

Alex felt a chill run down his spine. The Broker was unlike any adversary they had faced before. "We need to expose them," he said. "If we can show people who's really pulling the strings, we can turn the tide."

With renewed determination, Alex and Sarah launched a full-scale investigation into The Broker. They reached out to their network of allies, both old and new, gathering every piece of information they could find. It was painstaking work, but slowly, they began to piece together a picture of this elusive figure.

Their breakthrough came when they discovered a series of financial transactions linking The Broker to several high-profile individuals in Centerton. The money trails were intricate and well-hidden, but Sarah's sharp legal mind and Alex's investigative instincts helped them uncover the connections.

Armed with this new information, they prepared to go public. They knew it would be risky—The Broker would not take kindly to being exposed—but they had no choice. The truth had to come out.

They organized a press conference, inviting journalists and community members to hear their findings. As they stood before the crowd, Alex felt a surge of determination. This was their moment to shine a light on the darkness that had plagued their city.

Sarah began, her voice steady and clear. "Thank you all for coming. We have uncovered evidence of a shadowy figure, known as The Broker, who has been manipulating events in our city to maintain a stranglehold of corruption and power."

Alex stepped forward, presenting the financial documents they had uncovered. "These transactions link The Broker to several key figures in Centerton. This is a sophisticated operation, designed to undermine our efforts and keep the corrupt in power. But we will not be silenced."

The room buzzed with shock and disbelief as the audience absorbed the gravity of their revelations. Questions flew, and Alex and Sarah answered them with the confidence that came from knowing they were on the side of truth.

As the press conference ended, Alex and Sarah knew that they had struck a significant blow against The Broker. But they also understood that their fight was far from over. The unseen hand was still out there, and their adversary would not go down without a fight.

In the days that followed, the community rallied around them. Supporters came forward with new information, and public opinion began to shift back in their favor. The Broker's grip on Centerton was weakening, but Alex and Sarah remained vigilant.

They had learned that the pursuit of justice was a marathon, not a sprint. It required perseverance, resilience, and an unwavering commitment to the truth. The road ahead would be difficult, but they were ready to face it together.

The unseen hand had tried to undermine their efforts, but Alex Turner and Sarah Miller were more determined than ever to bring about change. They knew that their fight for justice was far from over, but they were prepared to continue their journey, no matter the cost. The people of Centerton needed them, and they would not rest until justice prevailed.

CHAPTER 10

THE PRICE OF JUSTICE

The sun had begun to set, casting long shadows over the city of Centerton. Detective Alex Turner and lawyer Sarah Miller sat on a park bench, the weight of their journey pressing down on them like the fading daylight. The pursuit of justice had taken its toll, and now, in the quiet moments between battles, they were forced to confront the sacrifices they had made along the way.

Alex stared at the horizon, lost in thought. The fight against corruption had consumed his life, leaving little room for anything else. He thought about the friends he had lost, those who had been unable to keep pace with his relentless drive. Relationships had strained and snapped under the pressure, leaving him more isolated than ever.

Sarah sensed his melancholy and placed a reassuring hand on his arm. "We've come a long way, Alex. But it hasn't been easy, has it?"

Alex shook his head, a bitter smile tugging at the corners of his mouth. "No, it hasn't. Sometimes I wonder if it's all worth it. The sleepless nights, the constant danger, the people we've lost along the way. We've paid a high price for this fight."

Sarah nodded, her own heart heavy with the weight of their sacrifices. She thought of the countless hours spent away from her family, the strain it had put on her marriage, the moments with her children that she could never get back. "It's been hard," she admitted. "But look at what we've accomplished. We've made a real difference. We've given people hope."

Their thoughts turned to those who had stood by them, only to fall victim to the very forces they were fighting. Marcus Rodriguez had been attacked in a dark alley, a warning from The Broker to back off. He had survived, but the incident had left him shaken and more cautious. Emily Harper had been harassed and threatened, forcing her to relocate and start anew.

"We've lost good people," Alex said quietly. "But we've also gained allies, and we've given a voice to those who were silenced. It's a hard balance to strike."

Sarah looked around the park, watching as children played and families enjoyed their evening together. "Justice isn't just about the big victories," she said. "It's about the everyday moments, the small changes that add up to something greater. We've seen that in the people we've helped, in the community we've built."

Alex nodded, understanding what she meant. They had seen the impact of their work firsthand—the neighborhoods revitalized, the corrupt officials held accountable, the renewed sense of trust in the justice system. It wasn't just about winning cases; it was about restoring faith in what was right and just.

"The price of justice is high," Sarah continued, her voice filled with conviction. "But it's a price worth paying. Because without it, we lose something fundamental—our sense of right and wrong, our belief that we can make a difference."

Alex took a deep breath, feeling a sense of resolve settle over him. "You're right. We've sacrificed a lot, but we've also gained so much. And we can't stop now. There's still so much work to do."

As they sat together, reflecting on their journey, they found strength in each other. They had faced unimaginable challenges, but they had also achieved incredible victories. Their sacrifices had not been in vain; they had made a real and lasting impact on Centerton.

"We need to keep pushing forward," Alex said, determination in his eyes. "For Marcus, for Emily, for everyone who's been hurt by this corruption. We owe it to them to see this through."

Sarah smiled, feeling a renewed sense of purpose. "And we will. Together, we'll continue this fight, no matter what it takes."

In the days that followed, Alex and Sarah redoubled their efforts. They worked tirelessly to expose The Broker, to bring justice to those who had been wronged, and to build a better future for their community. They knew the road ahead would be difficult, but they were ready to face it.

They rallied their allies, strengthening their network and fortifying their resolve. They reached out to new supporters, spreading their message and garnering more resources. The fight was far from over, but they were more determined than ever to see it through.

As they continued their journey, they kept the memories of those they had lost close to their hearts. Their sacrifices fueled their determination, reminding them of the high stakes and the importance of their mission. The price of justice was steep, but it was a price they were willing to pay.

In the heart of Centerton, where corruption had once thrived, a new dawn was breaking. The fight for justice had taken its toll, but Alex Turner and Sarah Miller stood resolute. They had faced the unseen hand and emerged stronger, more committed to their cause.

The price of justice was high, but as they looked out over their city, they knew it was worth it. For every sacrifice, there was a victory. For every loss, there was hope. And as long as they continued to stand up for what was right, they knew that justice would prevail.

The pursuit of justice was a never-ending journey, one that required courage, resilience, and an unwavering commitment to the truth. And as they moved forward, Alex and Sarah were ready to pay the price, knowing that their fight was not just for themselves, but for the future of Centerton and all who called it home.

CHAPTER 11

THE POWER OF UNITY

The fight for justice in Centerton had taken its toll on Detective Alex Turner and lawyer Sarah Miller, but it had also revealed a profound truth: they could not do it alone. The challenges they faced were too great, the adversaries too powerful. In the face of such adversity, they found strength in unity.

They began to forge alliances with like-minded individuals who shared their vision of a more just and equitable society. It started with Marcus Rodriguez, who, despite the attack he had suffered, remained determined to contribute to their cause. His street smarts and network of contacts proved invaluable.

One evening, as they gathered in Sarah's living room, they discussed the next steps. "We need more people," Sarah said, her tone resolute. "People who are willing to stand up and fight with us. We can't do this alone."

Alex agreed. "We've made a lot of progress, but The Broker is still out there, pulling strings. We need to build a coalition that can withstand their influence."

They reached out to community leaders, activists, and other professionals who had seen the impact of corruption firsthand. Their first major recruit was Jenny Huang, a passionate journalist who had been tirelessly reporting on the injustices in Centerton. Her investigative skills and media connections brought a new dimension to their efforts.

"I'm all in," Jenny said during their first meeting. "I've been covering this city's issues for years, and it's time to take a stand. We need to expose The Broker and their network."

Next, they connected with Dr. Samuel Ortega, a respected professor of political science at Centerton University. He had long been an advocate for transparency and good governance, and his expertise added a strategic edge to their movement.

"The power of change lies in education and awareness," Dr. Ortega stated. "We must not only fight the corruption but also educate our community about the importance of accountability and justice."

With each new ally, their coalition grew stronger. They organized town hall meetings, bringing together diverse groups to discuss the issues plaguing Centerton and brainstorm solutions. These meetings became a hub for activism and community engagement, fostering a sense of unity and shared purpose.

At one such meeting, Alex and Sarah stood before a crowded hall, filled with faces reflecting a mix of hope and determination. "Thank you all for being here," Alex began. "Our city is at a crossroads, and it's up to us to decide which path we take. Together, we have the power to bring about real change."

Sarah took over, her voice filled with conviction. "This fight is bigger than any one of us. It's about standing up for justice, for those who cannot stand up for themselves. We are stronger together, and together, we can overcome any obstacle."

The room erupted in applause, the energy palpable. People shared their stories, offered their skills, and pledged their support. The power of unity was evident, and it gave

Alex and Sarah the boost they needed to keep pushing forward.

Their coalition began to make significant strides. Jenny's articles brought national attention to their cause, Dr. Ortega's lectures mobilized students and academics, and Marcus's connections helped them gather crucial intelligence. They were a formidable team, each member playing a vital role in the movement.

One of their most significant victories came when they uncovered a major financial scandal linked to The Broker. Dr. Ortega's research, combined with Jenny's investigative prowess and Marcus's street-level insights, provided irrefutable evidence of embezzlement and fraud. The revelation shook Centerton to its core, leading to the arrest of several high-profile individuals and further weakening The Broker's grip on the city.

As they celebrated their success, Sarah reflected on their journey. "We've come so far," she said, looking around at her friends and allies. "This is what happens when we stand together. We're making a real difference."

Alex nodded, feeling a deep sense of pride and gratitude. "Unity is our greatest strength. We've proven that we're stronger together than we are apart. And we're not done yet."

With their coalition solidified and their resolve stronger than ever, Alex and Sarah continued their fight against corruption and injustice. They knew that there would be more challenges ahead, but they also knew that they had the power of unity on their side.

The power of unity became their rallying cry, inspiring others to join their cause. The movement grew, fueled by the collective determination to create a better, more just Centerton. They were a diverse group, but their shared vision bound them together, making them an unstoppable force.

As they marched forward, Alex and Sarah felt a renewed sense of hope. The fight for justice was far from over, but they were no longer fighting alone. With their allies by their side, they were ready to face whatever came next, knowing that together, they could achieve anything.

The power of unity had transformed their struggle into a movement, one that would continue to grow and thrive, bringing light to the darkest corners of Centerton. And as long as they stood united, they knew that justice would prevail.

CHAPTER 12

THE PATH FORWARD

The successes of their coalition had reinvigorated Alex Turner and Sarah Miller, filling them with a renewed sense of hope and purpose. They had seen firsthand the power of unity and the impact of their collective efforts. Now, as they charted a path forward, they knew the road ahead would be challenging, but they were more determined than ever to continue their fight for justice.

One crisp morning, Alex and Sarah gathered with their core team—Marcus, Jenny, and Dr. Ortega—in the community center that had become their headquarters. The room was abuzz with energy as they discussed their next steps.

"We've made significant progress," Alex began, his voice strong and confident. "But we can't afford to become complacent. The Broker and their network are still out there, and we need to keep the pressure on."

Sarah nodded in agreement. "We need to continue exposing corruption and advocating for change. But we also need to think about how we can create lasting improvements in our community. It's not just about taking down the bad guys; it's about building something better."

Dr. Ortega leaned forward, his eyes thoughtful. "Education is key. We need to empower our community with knowledge and resources. If people understand their rights and how to hold their leaders accountable, we can prevent corruption from taking root again."

Jenny added, "We also need to keep the public engaged. The media can be a powerful tool for change. We need to make sure our message reaches as many people as possible."

With a clear strategy in mind, they began to outline their initiatives. They decided to launch a series of community workshops focused on civic education, transparency, and good governance. These workshops would be held in various neighborhoods, making them accessible to as many people as possible.

Jenny would spearhead a media campaign to keep the spotlight on their efforts and highlight stories of positive change. Her articles and reports would continue to hold corrupt individuals accountable while showcasing the strength and resilience of the community.

Marcus would lead grassroots efforts, organizing volunteers and connecting with local organizations to ensure their initiatives reached those who needed them most. His connections and street-level insights would be invaluable in mobilizing support.

Dr. Ortega would collaborate with local schools and universities to integrate civic education into their curricula. By educating the next generation about the importance of integrity and accountability, they could foster a culture of transparency and justice.

As they laid out their plans, Alex felt a sense of optimism wash over him. They were not just reacting to corruption; they were proactively building a better future. Each step they took brought them closer to their goal of creating a just and equitable society.

Their first major initiative was a town hall meeting, where they would present their plans to the community and gather feedback. The event was held in the local high school auditorium, and the turnout was beyond their expectations. The room was filled with people eager to hear about the path forward.

Alex stood at the podium, looking out at the sea of faces. He felt a surge of pride and responsibility. "Thank you all for being here," he began. "We've made great strides in our fight against corruption, but we know there's still much work to be done. Today, we want to share our vision for the future and hear your thoughts on how we can achieve it together."

Sarah took over, outlining their initiatives and emphasizing the importance of community involvement. "This isn't just about us; it's about all of us. We need your help to make Centerton the place we know it can be. A place where justice prevails, and everyone has a voice."

The response was overwhelmingly positive. Community members offered ideas, volunteered their time, and expressed their commitment to the cause. The energy in the room was palpable, a testament to the power of unity and collective action.

In the weeks that followed, Alex and Sarah worked tirelessly to implement their plans. The community workshops were a resounding success, with attendees eager to learn and engage. Jenny's media campaign kept the public informed and motivated, while Dr. Ortega's educational initiatives began to take root in local schools.

Marcus's grassroots efforts brought together volunteers from all walks of life, creating a network of support that strengthened their movement. The coalition's initiatives began to bear fruit, fostering a sense of hope and renewal in the community.

As they continued their work, Alex and Sarah reflected on the journey that had brought them to this point. They had faced immense challenges and made significant sacrifices, but they had also achieved incredible victories. Their fight for justice had transformed from a personal mission into a powerful movement that was creating real, lasting change.

One evening, as they walked through a revitalized neighborhood, they marveled at the progress they had made. Children played in the streets, families gathered on porches, and a sense of community flourished.

"We've come a long way," Alex said, his voice filled with pride. "But we're not done yet. There's still so much more we can do."

Sarah nodded, her heart swelling with determination. "We've shown that change is possible, and we've inspired others to join us. The road ahead will be challenging, but I know we can overcome any obstacle if we stand together."

Their journey was far from over, but they faced the future with hope and resolve. Each step they took brought them closer to their goal of creating a better, more just society. They knew the path forward would be difficult, but they were ready for whatever challenges lay ahead.

In the heart of Centerton, where corruption had once thrived, a new era was dawning. Alex Turner and Sarah Miller, united in their fight for justice, were charting a path forward that would leave a lasting legacy for generations to come. The power of unity had shown them the way, and with each step, they moved closer to their vision of a brighter future.

CHAPTER 13

THE LEGACY OF JUSTICE

As the sun set over Centerton, casting a golden glow over the city, Detective Alex Turner and lawyer Sarah Miller found a quiet moment to reflect on their journey. They stood on the steps of the community center, the heart of their movement, watching as people came and went, their faces filled with hope and determination.

The fight for justice had been long and arduous, filled with setbacks and triumphs. But as they looked back on their journey, Alex and Sarah knew that their efforts had not been in vain. They had built something lasting, something that would continue to inspire others long after they were gone.

"It's hard to believe how far we've come," Alex said, his voice tinged with awe. "We started with just the two of us, and now look at this. We've created a movement, a community that stands up for what's right."

Sarah smiled, her eyes reflecting the pride she felt. "We have. And it's not just about the victories we've won. It's about the people we've inspired, the changes we've made. Our fight for justice has become something bigger than us."

They thought of the countless individuals who had joined their cause, each bringing their own strength and determination to the fight. People like Marcus Rodriguez, who had turned his life around and become a pillar of the community. Jenny Huang, whose relentless pursuit of the truth had shone a light on the darkest corners of Centerton. Dr. Samuel Ortega, whose educational initiatives were shaping the minds of future generations.

"Each one of them is part of our legacy," Alex continued. "They've taken up the mantle and carried it forward. That's what matters most. We've shown that change is possible, that justice can prevail."

Sarah nodded. "And it will continue to prevail, as long as there are people willing to stand up and fight for it. We've planted the seeds, and now it's up to others to nurture them."

Their thoughts turned to the impact their work had had on the community. The neighborhoods they had revitalized, the corrupt officials they had brought to justice, the renewed sense of trust in the justice system. They had given people hope and a belief in a brighter future.

"We've given them a voice," Sarah said softly. "We've shown them that they don't have to accept injustice, that they can make a difference. That's our legacy."

As they stood there, they were approached by a group of young people, their faces alight with enthusiasm. One of them, a teenage girl named Maya, stepped forward. She had been a regular attendee at their workshops and had recently started her own youth advocacy group.

"Alex, Sarah," Maya began, her voice filled with admiration. "I just wanted to thank you for everything you've done. You've inspired us so much. We're going to keep fighting for justice, just like you taught us."

Sarah's heart swelled with pride. "Thank you, Maya. You and your friends are the future. It's up to you to continue the work we've started. And I have no doubt that you will."

Maya beamed. "We won't let you down. We promise."

As the young people walked away, Alex turned to Sarah, his eyes filled with emotion. "That's what it's all about, isn't it? Inspiring the next generation, giving them the tools and the courage to keep fighting."

Sarah squeezed his hand. "Yes, it is. And knowing that we've done that, that we've made a difference, makes all the sacrifices worth it."

Their journey was nearing its end, but the legacy they had built would endure. Their fight for justice had become a beacon of hope, a testament to the power of courage, resilience, and unwavering commitment to the truth.

In the days that followed, Alex and Sarah continued their work, each step bringing them closer to the culmination of their efforts. They knew that their time in the spotlight was drawing to a close, but they were content knowing that they had laid a strong foundation for others to build upon.

As they prepared for their final public address, they took a moment to reflect on the journey that had brought them here. They had faced immense challenges and made significant sacrifices, but they had also achieved incredible victories. Their fight for justice had transformed from a personal mission into a powerful movement that would continue to inspire others for years to come.

On the day of their address, the community center was filled to capacity. People from all walks of life had come to hear Alex and Sarah speak one last time. The air was charged with anticipation and gratitude, a testament to the impact they had made.

Alex stepped up to the podium, looking out at the faces of the people they had fought for and alongside. "Thank you all for being here," he began, his voice steady and strong. "This journey has been one of the most challenging and rewarding experiences of our lives. We've faced obstacles that seemed insurmountable, but together, we've overcome them."

Sarah joined him, her eyes shining with pride. "Our fight for justice has always been about more than just winning cases. It's been about standing up for what's right, about giving a voice to the voiceless, and about creating a community that believes in the power of truth. And that's what we've done—together."

The crowd erupted in applause, their cheers echoing through the room. Alex and Sarah took a moment to soak in the energy and the gratitude that filled the air.

"We may be stepping back," Alex continued, "but the fight for justice will go on. It will go on in each and every one of you. You are the torchbearers now. It's up to you to continue this work, to keep standing up and speaking out against injustice."

Sarah nodded, her voice filled with emotion. "We have faith in you. We believe in you. And we know that you will carry this legacy forward. Thank you for standing with us, for fighting with us, and for believing in the power of justice."

As they stepped down from the podium, the crowd surged forward, eager to thank them, to share their own stories of inspiration, and to pledge their continued commitment to the cause.

In that moment, Alex and Sarah knew that their legacy was secure. They had built something lasting, something that would continue to grow and inspire others long after they were gone. Their journey had been one of courage, resilience, and unwavering commitment to the truth.

As they walked out of the community center, hand in hand, they felt a profound sense of peace. The fight for justice would never truly be over, but they had made a difference. They had inspired others to stand up and speak out, to believe in the power of truth and the possibility of change.

CHAPTER 14

THE FINAL STAND

The air was thick with tension as Detective Alex Turner and lawyer Sarah Miller prepared for what they knew would be their final stand against the forces of corruption and injustice that had long plagued Centerton. This was the culmination of years of hard work, sacrifice, and relentless pursuit of truth. Their adversaries were formidable, but they could not afford to back down now. With the support of their allies and the unwavering belief in their cause, they stood firm in their resolve to see justice done.

It began with a tip from an anonymous source—an insider willing to expose the final, crucial piece of evidence that would bring down The Broker and their entire network. The tip led them to a high-stakes meeting scheduled to take place in a secluded warehouse on the outskirts of the city. It was a meeting where the city's most corrupt officials and business leaders would finalize their latest scheme, one that would solidify their control over Centerton.

The team gathered in the community center, their nerves on edge but their spirits high. Alex, Sarah, Marcus Rodriguez, Jenny Huang, Dr. Samuel Ortega, and a group of trusted allies formed a tight circle, going over their plan one last time.

"We have one shot at this," Alex said, his voice steady but intense. "This is the moment we've been working towards. We can't let them get away."

Sarah nodded, her determination mirrored in the faces of their allies. "We've come too far to fail now. We have the evidence, we have the support, and most importantly, we have the truth on our side. Let's finish this."

As they moved into position, the gravity of the situation settled over them. The warehouse was heavily guarded, and the risk was high. But they had prepared meticulously, coordinating with law enforcement and ensuring that they had the legal backing to take down everyone involved.

Jenny and Dr. Ortega had been instrumental in rallying public support and keeping the media informed. The press was ready to cover the event as soon as it unfolded, ensuring that the truth would be broadcast far and wide.

Under the cover of darkness, Alex and Sarah led their team to the warehouse. The tension was palpable as they approached, their senses heightened by the knowledge that this was it—the final showdown. They moved with precision and caution, taking care not to alert the guards prematurely.

Inside the warehouse, the meeting was underway. The Broker, a shadowy figure who had orchestrated the city's corruption from behind the scenes, sat at the head of a long table. Around them were the city's most powerful and corrupt individuals, their faces twisted with greed and arrogance.

Alex signaled to his team, and they moved into action. Law enforcement, led by officers who had remained loyal to the cause of justice, stormed the warehouse, quickly securing the exits and apprehending the guards. The corrupt officials and business leaders were caught off guard, their faces turning pale as the reality of the situation set in.

"The game is over," Alex announced, stepping forward with Sarah at his side. "You're all under arrest for conspiracy, fraud, and corruption. We have the evidence, and we have the witnesses. It's time to face justice."

The Broker stood, their eyes narrowing as they tried to maintain control. "You think this will change anything? There will always be someone else to take my place."

Sarah met their gaze, her voice calm but resolute. "Maybe. But as long as there are people willing to stand up and fight, people willing to expose the truth and hold the powerful accountable, there will always be hope. Your reign ends here."

As the law enforcement officers moved in to make the arrests, the tension in the room broke. The corrupt officials and business leaders were led away in handcuffs, their protests and threats falling on deaf ears. The Broker, the mastermind behind the city's corruption, was finally unmasked and taken into custody.

Outside the warehouse, the media had gathered, ready to broadcast the news. Jenny Huang stood ready with her camera crew, capturing the moment for posterity. Dr. Ortega addressed the crowd that had gathered, speaking passionately about the importance of integrity, transparency, and the rule of law.

Alex and Sarah emerged from the warehouse, their faces reflecting a mixture of relief and triumph. They had faced their greatest challenge and emerged victorious. The fight had been long and arduous, but they had succeeded in bringing down the forces of corruption and injustice that had plagued their city.

As they stood before the cameras, Alex spoke to the crowd. "This victory belongs to all of us. It belongs to the people who have stood up and spoken out, to those who have risked everything for the sake of justice. We have shown that, together, we can make a difference."

Sarah added, "This is not the end of our journey. It's the beginning of a new chapter for Centerton. A chapter where justice prevails, where truth is valued, and where every individual has a voice. We will continue to fight for this vision, and we invite all of you to join us."

The crowd erupted in applause, their cheers echoing through the night. The legacy of their fight for justice was secure, and their message was clear: no matter the challenges, no matter the adversaries, the power of unity and the truth would always prevail.

As the night wore on, Alex and Sarah found a moment of quiet amidst the celebration. They stood together, reflecting on the journey that had brought them to this point.

"We did it," Alex said, his voice filled with emotion. "We really did it."

Sarah nodded, her eyes shining with pride. "Yes, we did. And this is just the beginning. There's so much more to do, but we've proven that we can make a difference."

Together, they faced the future with hope and determination. Their final stand against corruption and injustice had been successful, and they knew that they would continue to fight for a better, more just world. The power of truth and the strength of their unity would guide them forward, inspiring others to join their cause and carry on the legacy of justice they had built.

CHAPTER 15

THE DAWN OF A NEW ERA

The first rays of sunlight crept over the horizon, casting a warm glow over the city of Centerton. For Detective Alex Turner and lawyer Sarah Miller, it marked the beginning of a new era. The forces of corruption had been defeated, and justice had prevailed. But as they stood together, looking out over their city, they knew that their journey was far from over.

The past months had been a whirlwind of activity. The arrests of The Broker and their network had sent shockwaves through Centerton, leading to a series of reforms and a renewed focus on transparency and accountability. The community had rallied together, inspired by the victory and determined to build a brighter future.

Alex and Sarah had become symbols of hope and resilience, their tireless efforts serving as a testament to the power of unity and the importance of standing up for what is right. Their faces had been splashed across newspapers and television screens, their story told and retold. But for them, it wasn't about the accolades—it was about the impact they had made and the lives they had touched.

As they stood on the steps of the community center, watching the city come to life, Sarah turned to Alex. "We've come a long way, haven't we?"

Alex nodded, a smile tugging at the corners of his mouth. "We have. It's been a tough journey, but it's all been worth it. Look at what we've accomplished."

The streets below were bustling with activity. Families were out for morning walks, children played in the parks, and local businesses thrived. There was a palpable sense of optimism in the air, a feeling that Centerton was on the cusp of something great.

But Alex and Sarah knew that their work was not done. The pursuit of justice was a never-ending journey, one that required constant vigilance and unwavering commitment. They had achieved a significant victory, but there would always be new challenges, new threats to the integrity of their community.

"We can't let our guard down," Sarah said, her expression serious. "There will always be those who seek to do wrong, to exploit others for their own gain. We have to stay vigilant."

Alex agreed. "Absolutely. We've built a strong foundation, but we need to keep building, keep fighting. We need to ensure that the reforms we've started are maintained and that the people of Centerton continue to feel empowered and heard."

Their coalition had grown stronger, their network of allies more extensive. They had forged partnerships with local organizations, schools, and businesses, all dedicated to the cause of justice. The community workshops and educational programs had become a staple, fostering a culture of integrity and accountability.

As they walked through the city, they were greeted with smiles and words of gratitude. People stopped to thank them, to share their own stories of how the fight against corruption had changed their lives. It was a reminder of why they had started this journey in the first place and why they could never give up.

They visited the newly established Justice Center, a symbol of the progress they had made. The center served as a hub for legal aid, civic education, and community engagement. It was a place where people could come for help, where they could learn about their rights and how to stand up against injustice.

Inside, they were met by Marcus Rodriguez, now a key figure at the center, who had dedicated himself to helping others turn their lives around. "Alex, Sarah," he greeted them warmly. "It's great to see you. The center has been a huge success. We're making a real difference."

Jenny Huang was also there, working on an investigative piece about the ongoing reforms. "We've come a long way," she said with a smile. "But there's still so much to do. I'm glad we're all in this together."

Dr. Samuel Ortega joined them, his eyes shining with pride. "Education is the key to lasting change," he said. "And we're seeing the results of our efforts. The next generation is more informed, more engaged, and more determined to uphold justice."

As they stood together, Alex and Sarah felt a profound sense of fulfillment. They had faced immense challenges and made significant sacrifices, but they had also achieved incredible victories. Their journey had been one of courage, resilience, and unwavering commitment to the truth.

The sun continued to rise, casting a new light on Centerton. The dawn of a new era had arrived, one filled with hope and promise. Alex and Sarah knew that the fight for justice would never truly end, but they were ready to face whatever challenges lay ahead.

"We've done good work," Alex said, his voice filled with determination. "But there's always more to be done. We need to stay vigilant, stay committed."

Sarah nodded, her eyes filled with resolve. "As long as there are people who seek to do wrong, we'll be here to stand up and fight for what's right."

They had created a legacy of justice, one that would inspire others to continue the fight. And as they looked out over their city, they felt a deep sense of pride and gratitude. They had made a difference, and they would continue to do so, one step at a time.

The pursuit of justice was a never-ending journey, but it was one they were willing to take. With the support of their allies and the power of truth on their side, they knew they could overcome any obstacle. The dawn of a new era had arrived, and with it, the promise of a brighter future for Centerton.

As they walked hand in hand, ready to face whatever lay ahead, Alex and Sarah knew that their work was far from over. But they were prepared, now more than ever, to continue their fight for justice, to protect the values they held dear, and to ensure that Centerton remained a beacon of hope and integrity.

The journey would continue, and they would be there every step of the way, standing up for what was right, no matter the cost. The dawn of a new era had begun, and with it, the unyielding promise that justice would always prevail.

A BEACON OF HOPE

The sun set over Centerton, casting a golden hue across the skyline, symbolizing the end of one chapter and the beginning of another. Alex Turner and Sarah Miller stood together on the rooftop of the Justice Center, reflecting on their journey and the battles they had fought. The city below was a testament to their resilience, a community transformed by their unwavering commitment to justice.

In the months following their final stand against corruption, Centerton had begun to heal. The reforms implemented had taken root, and the spirit of integrity and accountability was becoming a defining characteristic of the city. The Justice Center had become a beacon of hope, a place where people could come for help, guidance, and a sense of community.

Alex and Sarah had faced immense challenges, from personal sacrifices to confronting deeply entrenched corruption. Yet, through it all, they had remained steadfast in their belief that justice was worth fighting for. Their journey had been one of transformation, not just for Centerton, but for themselves as well.

As they looked out over the city, they saw the fruits of their labor. Schools were teaching the next generation about the importance of integrity and civic responsibility. Local businesses were thriving under the fair and transparent regulations that had been put in place. The community had rallied together, united in their commitment to uphold the values that Alex and Sarah had championed.

"Can you believe how far we've come?" Sarah asked, a hint of awe in her voice.

Alex smiled, nodding. "It's incredible. But we didn't do it alone. The people of this city stood with us every step of the way."

Their thoughts turned to the allies they had made along their journey—Marcus Rodriguez, Jenny Huang, Dr. Samuel Ortega, and countless others who had played vital roles in their fight for justice. Each of them had contributed to the transformation of Centerton, proving that real change was possible when people worked together towards a common goal.

"Do you think we'll ever truly be done?" Sarah asked, her gaze fixed on the horizon.

Alex shook his head. "Justice is a continuous pursuit. There will always be new challenges, new battles to fight. But we've shown that we can make a difference, and that's what matters."

Sarah nodded in agreement. "It's not about the destination, but the journey. As long as we keep moving forward, keep fighting for what's right, we'll make this world a better place."

Their journey had been marked by victories and setbacks, by moments of doubt and unwavering determination. They had faced corruption, deceit, and the harsh realities of a flawed system, yet they had emerged stronger, more resolute in their mission.

As the night settled in, Alex and Sarah knew that their work was far from over. The pursuit of justice was a never-ending journey, one that required constant vigilance and a deep-seated commitment to truth and integrity. But they were ready. They had faced the darkness and come out stronger, their resolve unshakable.

The city of Centerton stood as a testament to their efforts, a beacon of hope in a world often overshadowed by injustice. Alex and Sarah had proven that change was possible, that one could stand against corruption and emerge victorious. Their legacy would inspire others to continue the fight, to stand up for what was right, no matter the cost.

As they turned to leave the rooftop, their hearts were filled with hope and determination. They knew that the road ahead would be challenging, but they were ready to face it together. Their journey had just begun, and they were prepared to walk the path of justice for as long as it took.

Centerton was a city reborn, a community united by a common purpose. And as long as there were people like Alex and Sarah, willing to fight for what was right, there would always be hope. The dawn of a new era had arrived, and with it, the promise of a brighter future for all.

And so, with the city lights shining brightly below, Alex and Sarah stepped into the future, ready to continue their fight for justice, to protect the values they held dear, and to ensure that Centerton remained a beacon of hope and integrity for generations to come.

To be continued – Part 4

www.ingramcontent.com/pod-product-compliance
Lightning Source LLC
Chambersburg PA
CBHW010425120726
47992CB00008B/3328